Chocolate Dreams

Candy Fairies

Chocolate Dreams

HELEN PERELMAN

ILLUSTRATED BY

ERICA-JANE WATERS

SCHOLASTIC INC.

ISBN 978-1-338-12643-3

Text copyright © 2010 by Helen Perelman. Illustrations copyright © 2010 by Erica-Jane Waters. All rights reserved. Published by Scholastic Inc., 557 Broadway, New York, NY 10012, by arrangement with Aladdin Paperbacks, an imprint of Simon & Schuster Children's Publishing Division. SCHOLASTIC and associated logos are trademarks and/or registered trademarks of Scholastic Inc.

The publisher does not have any control over and does not assume any responsibility for author or third-party websites or their content.

12 11 10 9 8 7 6 5 4 3 2 1   16 17 18 19 20 21

Printed in the U.S.A.   40

First Scholastic printing, October 2016

Designed by Karin Paprocki
The text of this book was set in Berthold Baskerville Book.

For Samantha and Rachel,

who are deliciously fun

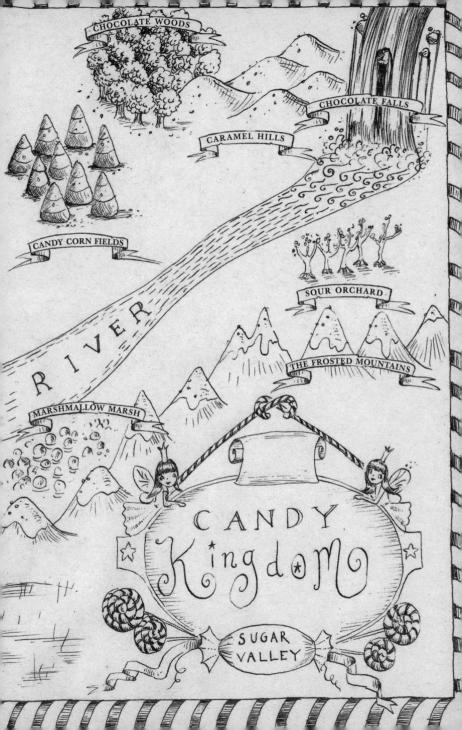

Contents

Chocolate Dreams

CHAPTER 1

Sweet Spring

Wait for me!" Cocoa the Chocolate Fairy called. She fluttered her wings and flew after her friend.

"Come on," Melli cried over her shoulder. Her caramel-colored dress sparkled in the sunlight. "Let's go!" Her purple wings flapped quickly as she soared ahead.

Cocoa took a deep breath as she caught up to her friend. The smell of chocolate from the roaring Chocolate River made her smile. This was her favorite spot in the entire Candy Kingdom.

Everything looked delicious this bright morning. The morning sun sprinkled light over colorful Sugar Valley. Spring was the most glorious season in the kingdom. All the candy flowers and trees were in bloom, and fairies everywhere were celebrating. A new season of candy had begun!

Cocoa spotted their friends on the sugar banks of the Chocolate River. Raina was easy to see with her bright red wings. And next to her was tiny Dash in her white shimmering dress and her small silver wings.

"There they are!" Cocoa said, pointing. She sailed down close to the river. All the new chocolate flowers were sprouting up along the shoreline. Chocolate wildflowers were always so sweet and colorful!

What a choc-o-rific morning, she thought.

"What took you so long?" Dash asked when she saw her friends. The tiny Mint Fairy might have been one of the smallest fairies in Sugar Valley, but she was also the fastest. And not always the most patient!

Cocoa came to a landing beside her friends. She pointed to the east side of the kingdom, where she and Melli lived. "We had the longest distance to fly," Cocoa said. "Besides, we're not *that* late. Berry isn't even here yet."

"Oh, peppermint sticks!" Dash exclaimed. "Berry's always late."

Berry was a Fruit Fairy who always took her sweet time getting ready. She liked everything perfect, from her hair to her toenails. By far, she was one of the most glamorous fairies in Sugar Valley. But she was a very good friend.

Raina patted a spot next to her on the white sugar sand. "Come, sit down, Cocoa," the Gummy Fairy said kindly. "You must be tired."

All Gummy Fairies had a gentle spirit. Their spirit helped them with the difficult task of watching over Gummy Forest. Growing gummy crops and tending to the gummy animals was hard work. But Raina had proved to have the most patience. She was the Gummy Fairy in charge of the gummy animals in Gummy Forest. Even with the pesky gummy worms and mischievous gummy fish, Raina never lost her cool. But above all, she didn't like messes—or fights with her friends.

"I brought you all something," Melli said cheerfully. She reached into her bag and pulled out caramel sticks. "Fresh caramel!" she exclaimed. She handed one to each of her friends.

"Delicious," Dash exclaimed. She was tiny, but she was always hungry! She loved the thick caramel sticks that grew at the top of Caramel Hills. All Caramel Fairies were able to make caramel, but Dash knew that Melli's sweet touch and generous heart made these caramels the best in the kingdom.

"Thank you!" Cocoa said. "I'm starving. I've been rolling chocolate eggs all morning." She

took a bite of the sweet stalk. "Did you know that each egg has to be turned every hour?" She looked around at her friends.

"We know," Melli said playfully. She couldn't help but gently tease her friend. "To get the eggs the perfect shape, they need to be turned every hour." She grinned. Cocoa had been telling them that for weeks now!

Every spring one Chocolate Fairy was chosen to care for the first spring chocolate eggs. This year Cocoa was that proud fairy.

On the first day of spring Cocoa would deliver the eggs to Candy Castle. Royal Foil Fairies worked all winter to create beautiful foil to decorate the eggs for the Egg Parade.

The parade of chocolates moved through Sugar Valley and was a joyous event. There were floats full of chocolates for all to view. But everyone waited to see the delicate sugar basket filled with the foil-wrapped eggs. The eggs were presented to the fairy princess in the Royal Gardens of Candy Castle. A glorious chocolate feast was held afterward to celebrate. All the fairies looked forward to the festive event.

"It is a big honor to be in charge of the eggs," Melli said. She stood up and walked over to the proud Chocolate Fairy. "And, Cocoa, you are doing a great job."

Cocoa smiled. "Thanks." She stood up with her hands on her hips, and spread her golden wings. "The eggs are getting big already!" she boasted.

"Big enough?" Dash asked. "Bigger than me?"

Her minty nature definitely gave her a cool attitude.

"The eggs need to get bigger," Cocoa replied. "And they will. These are the first spring chocolates." Cocoa fluttered her wings. "This is going to be the best crop of eggs Candy Kingdom has ever seen. You can be sure as sugar that they'll be the biggest and best yet!"

2

A Big Chocolate Surprise

Cocoa leaned back and looked up at the sky. She loved being with her friends—and taking a rest from watching the eggs! She bit another chunk out of her caramel stalk. "After these eggs are delivered to the castle, I'm going to sleep for a whole day!"

"Hey, lazy wings!" Berry called cheerfully from the air. She gracefully landed next to Cocoa on the sugar sand. The beautiful Fruit Fairy smoothed out her raspberry-colored dress. "What are you fairies up to this delicious morning?"

"Waiting for you," Cocoa said, rolling her eyes. "What else is new?"

"What's got your wings all in a tangle?" Berry asked. "I'm right on time."

Raina stood up. "Well, we're all here now," she said kindly. She grinned at her friends. "And that is what's important."

"That's true," Melli said. "Let's have some fun!"

The five fairies ate their caramels and talked about the upcoming Egg Parade.

"I'm going to wear a chocolate-leaf crown," Cocoa declared. "I've already started to look for the best leaves."

"And I'm going to wear a new fruit-chew necklace," Berry said. She dug her hand into her pocket to show the sparkling sugar-coated jewels. "I just picked them yesterday." She held out her hand to show her friends.

"Oh, Berry!" Melli cried. "Those are beautiful. You have the best taste."

"They'll make a really nice necklace," Dash told her. She peered into her friend's hand. "But they certainly look good enough to eat!"

Cocoa laughed. "Berry, you'd better hide those from Dash. You always know how to dress up an outfit with delicious treats."

"A fairy has to know how to accessorize!"

Berry said, grinning. She touched her head. Sparkly sugar clips held her dark, thick hair up in a perfect bun. "There are some great new fashions this spring," she added.

"That's for sure," Raina told her. "Everything about spring is so sweet, isn't it?"

"You say that about every season," Dash kidded her. She flew up to a chocolate flower, plucked it, and dipped her hand into the gooey mint center. "But I have to agree. These spring flowers are very good!"

"Mmm, let me have a taste," Melli said. She flew over to Dash and took a piece of the fresh flower. "You are right," she said, licking her fingers. "These are good."

Raina stood up and faced Gummy Forest. A gentle wind ruffled her red wings. She closed

her eyes. "I have to get back to the forest," she said.

"Will you be at Sun Dip later on?" Melli asked.

Sun Dip was a special time when the sun dipped below the Frosted Mountains, casting a beautiful evening light on the valley. All the fairies in Sugar Valley gathered to feast on their candy crops before they settled in for the night. It was the best part of the day!

"Can't wait!" Cocoa exclaimed, spreading her wings to fly.

"Wouldn't miss it," Dash shouted.

"Me too," Raina and Berry said at the same time.

Cocoa and Melli took off together for the eastern part of Sugar Valley. They waved good-bye to Berry, Dash, and Raina. Together, they flew back up Chocolate River, over Lollipop Landing, and to Chocolate Woods.

"Don't forget the caramel corn," Cocoa said. "We can dip them in chocolate tonight. I'll bring a bucket from Chocolate Falls. We can make chocolate dip surprises for everyone. It will be fun!"

"Sounds good," Melli answered. "I won't forget."

"Race you!" Cocoa shouted as she soared into Chocolate Woods. She loved a race! Skillfully, she dodged in and around the tall trees and quickly pulled ahead of Melli.

As she flew toward the rumbling of Chocolate Falls, Cocoa's eyes grew wide with fear. Just before Melli had to turn off for Caramel Hills, Cocoa gasped.

"Oh, sweet sugar!" Cocoa cried. She pointed to the chocolate egg nest on top of the tallest chocolate oak tree. The nest was empty! The chocolate eggs were gone!

CHAPTER 3

A Chocolate Mess

Cocoa couldn't believe her eyes. She flew over the empty chocolate nest. Where could the eggs have gone?

Maybe this is just a bad dream, she thought. She blinked her large brown eyes, but the nest was still bare! Her heart pounded in her chest. She shouldn't have left the eggs alone! But she never thought anything would happen to them. . . .

"The eggs!" Melli exclaimed. She touched down on the edge of the nest next to Cocoa. Her purple wings flapped quickly.

Cocoa shook her head. The whole kingdom was counting on her to deliver the chocolate eggs for the Egg Parade. And now she'd let everyone down.

A few weeks ago Fairy Princess Lolli had flown to Chocolate Woods and picked Cocoa to watch over the eggs. Cocoa had felt so special! In front of everyone in Chocolate Woods, she had made a promise to care for the eggs.

Having the royal fairy princess come to her home had been such a special treat. Everyone loved the beautiful fairy princess. Princess Lolli had a heart of sugar and was fair and true. She

cared for all the Candy Fairies and made Sugar Valley the sweetest place to live.

Princess Lolli will be so disappointed! Cocoa thought. She didn't want to upset the fairy princess. Not to mention the Royal Foil Fairies who were hard at work painting the elaborate wrappers for the eggs!

All her chocolate dreams were melting away.

"This is all my fault!" Cocoa cried. "No fairy has ever lost the chocolate eggs."

"Maybe they just rolled out?" Melli said hopefully. Melli always tried to see the bright side, but Cocoa couldn't see one at the moment.

Cocoa flew below the heavy branches of the chocolate oak tree. She knew eggs falling from the nest would be very unlikely. The nest was woven from the strongest chocolate branches.

Each one had been carefully picked. The idea of the eggs slipping or falling out didn't seem possible.

"Melli, they're not here," Cocoa whispered. "The Egg Parade is in two days. I can't create new eggs in time!"

Chocolate Fairies had chocolate magic. They could create chocolate candy with a simple touch. But unlike regular chocolate eggs, the spring eggs needed time to grow. Everyone in the kingdom counted on those eggs being in the Egg Parade. They needed to be extra-special!

"Let's keep looking, then," Melli said. She smiled at her friend. "I'm sure we'll find them."

Cocoa and Melli carefully searched Chocolate Woods. The bushes and trees were bursting with chocolates, and the rich, dark soil smelled

delicious. But there were no eggs anywhere . . .
not even a clue.

The two fairies flew in and out of the rows of
trees looking for any sign of the eggs.

"Let's check under the chocolate chip bushes,"
Melli told Cocoa. She pointed to the low, prickly
bushes around the old chocolate oak tree.

"I guess it is possible that they rolled under
there," Cocoa said. She was willing to look
anywhere for the precious eggs.

The short twig branches of the chocolate chip
bushes tickled Cocoa's wings, but she crawled
under several of them anyway.

"Melli, what am I going to do?" Cocoa cried.
Tears were in her eyes. She sat at the bottom of
the old chocolate oak. Her wings rubbed against
the rough chocolate bark. "Everyone was counting

on me! How could this have happened?"

"It's not your fault," Melli told her. "Come, quick." She pulled Cocoa's hand. "Let's cover the nest before anyone sees." She put her hand on Cocoa's shoulder. "That will give us time to figure something out."

Together, the two fairies pulled three large chocolate leaves over the nest. As they covered the nest, Cocoa thought about her morning. She had checked on the eggs and rolled them. The morning was no different from any other in the past few weeks. This was a real mystery. Or was it?

When the nest was covered, Cocoa looked up at her friend. "Melli," she said softly, "do you think someone *stole* the eggs?"

As a young fairy, Cocoa had heard stories

about candy stealing. But those were just fairy tales. She had never heard of chocolate eggs being stolen from their nest! And so close to the Egg Parade!

"Stolen?" Melli gasped. She had also heard the stories, but she thought that's all they were—stories. "You don't really believe all those fairy stories, do you?"

"But how else do we explain this?" Cocoa exclaimed.

"I suppose someone *could* have stolen the eggs," Melli said. She thought about that idea for a moment. "But who would steal the spring eggs?" she wondered out loud. "Who would do such a sour thing?"

Cocoa shuddered. She immediately knew the answer to Melli's question. There was only one creature sour enough in Sugar Valley. Her wings twitched. She didn't want to say what she was thinking.

"We're going to need more help," Melli said. She fluttered her wings nervously. "Raina, Berry, and Dash will know what to do. I'll send word for them to meet us here."

As Melli sent a sugar fly to deliver the messages, Cocoa sat with her head hanging low. She wanted to believe that her friends could help her. But this was a huge problem. This was one huge chocolate mess.

More than anything, Cocoa wanted to make this situation right. She'd need every ounce of chocolate courage she had. She hoped her friends would get there soon.

CHAPTER

4

A Sour Sight

Raina was worried. The message from Melli didn't make sense to her. How could the chocolate eggs be missing? The sugar fly that delivered the message had also told her to find Berry and fly as fast as they could to Chocolate Woods. Sugar flies only delivered short messages, so she'd have to wait until she saw Cocoa to get the whole story.

As fast as she could, Raina flew to Lollipop Landing. She spotted Berry right away, putting the finishing touches on her cherry lollipops.

"Berry!" Raina called. She flew up to her and grabbed her arm.

Berry was surprised to see her friend. But as soon as she saw her, Berry knew something was wrong. Raina's worried expression and her shivering wings made Berry concerned. When Raina told her what had happened, Berry left her lollipops and they flew off to Chocolate Woods.

Cocoa needed them. And the two Candy Fairies were on their way.

"I don't understand," Berry said. She was soaring through the air as fast as she could. "Chocolate eggs *don't* disappear."

"No, they don't," Raina said, agreeing. "All of Candy Kingdom is waiting for those eggs—and the Egg Parade! Spring isn't official until those eggs are delivered!"

"The sugar fly didn't say anything else?" Berry asked. She knew that Raina often overreacted. But in this case, she understood. Missing chocolate eggs were something to be very concerned about.

"No, he had no other information," Raina said. "The fly just delivered the message and then flew off. He was off to Peppermint Grove to find Dash next."

Raina took a deep breath. *This isn't good news*, she said to herself. She thought of her friend, and shook her head. "Poor Cocoa!" she cried.

The two fairies flew up along Chocolate

River to Chocolate Woods. Raina glanced down at the roaring river. She put her hand up to her eyes to shield the glare from the sun. Was she imagining things? She shook her head and then looked down below again. She slowed her wings and pointed to the river.

"Berry!" she cried in a hushed whisper. "Look!"

Following Raina's finger, Berry looked down below. She squinted her blue eyes as she watched the scene.

"Come on! Let's get closer!" Berry said. She quickly dove down to get a better look at the river. As she flew closer, she saw what had caught Raina's eye. Hiding behind a large wild fruit-chew bush, she and Raina watched carefully. Furry little Chuchies were crossing the river. They were carrying a black licorice stretcher filled with Cocoa's chocolate eggs!

The Chuchies lived in the salty pretzel stalks near Black Licorice Swamp. Although they lived in the swamp, they loved fairy candy. The Chuchies were sneaky creatures who would do anything to get it!

Raina peered over Berry's shoulder in disbelief. "I've never seen the Chuchies in Candy Kingdom!" she whispered.

"Mogu!" Berry whispered to her. She narrowed her eyes. This bitterness could only come from one Sugar Valley creature. Just thinking of him made her scowl.

Raina gasped. Hearing that name sent a chill down to the tips of her wings. Mogu was a salty old troll who lived under the bridge in Black

Licorice Swamp. His sour nature was part of what made the swamp bitter and dark.

"You know that the Chuchies do whatever Mogu asks because he gives them candy," Berry said.

"*Stolen* candy," Raina said.

The old troll usually kept to himself and stayed under his bridge. But he was known to have candy cravings. . . .

But would he stoop to stealing? Raina wondered.

"Those furry little thieves never act alone," Berry said. She squinted her eyes as she watched. "They do whatever old Mogu tells them to do. He must be behind this!"

This situation was worse than Raina could have imagined. Nowhere in the Fairy Code Book was there any information about getting chocolate eggs back from Black Licorice Swamp! She watched as the Chuchies waddled across the river. There was nothing the two fairies could do. Candy Fairies had limited power across the river.

This was a very sour situation!

"What are we going to do?" Raina cried. Her wings started to twitch nervously.

"First, you have to calm down," Berry instructed. She looked Raina in the eye. "We have to tell Cocoa." Then she turned to watch the Chuchies cross the river. "Those rotten little thieves," she grumbled. "How dare they steal fairy chocolate!"

"But, Berry," Raina pleaded, "if you tell Cocoa that we saw the Chuchies with the eggs, she'll want to go see Mogu herself!" She shook her head, making her long hair fly in the breeze. "She's crazy enough to make that journey across the river and over the Frosted Mountains. We can't let her do that!"

Berry nodded her head, agreeing. "It would be just like Cocoa," she said. "But we have to tell her the truth. Someone needs to save the eggs. Now that the Chuchies took them across the river, we have to do something. Fast."

"I was afraid you were going to say that," Raina said.

5

Bittersweet News

Raina and Berry found Cocoa and Melli sitting at the bottom of the old chocolate oak tree.

"This is the gooiest mess of all time," Cocoa said. When she saw her friends coming, she looked up at them. Seeing them gave her a little bit of hope. She was glad her friends were there. "What am I going to do?" she cried.

"Mogu has the eggs," Berry told her before her feet even touched the ground. Berry always told things straight, and this news was too big to sugarcoat.

"Mogu!" Cocoa exclaimed. "That salty old troll! I knew it!"

Melli's mouth dropped open. "What?!"

"We saw the eggs," Berry went on. She moved closer to Cocoa. "They are safe," she said. Then she added, "For now."

"Holy peppermint!" Dash cried as she swooped into the Chocolate Woods. She was a bundle of excited energy. "Was that sugar fly for real? Are the eggs really gone?"

"Shhh," Melli scolded. She reached up and grabbed Dash's tiny hand. "We don't need every fairy in the kingdom to hear." She turned back to

Berry. "What are you talking about? Where did you see the eggs?"

Berry watched the look on each of her friends' faces. She was used to fairies gawking at her. Fairies usually stopped her to admire her beautiful wings or clothes, but this was different. This was serious. "Raina and I saw the Chuchies carrying the eggs over Chocolate River. They had a stretcher made out of black licorice."

Melli, Dash, and Cocoa gasped.

"Are you sure?" Melli asked Raina and Berry.

Raina quickly nodded her head. "They were Chuchies, all right. And they must have been following Mogu's orders, as usual." She rushed over to Cocoa. "Oh, Cocoa!" she cried. "I am so sorry!"

"We've got to do something!" Dash blurted.

Cocoa twirled her finger around one of her long curls. "I need to go get those eggs back!" She stood up and looked at her friends. They all looked shocked. "I can do it. I can trick that sour old troll!" she said. She stomped her foot. "He'd better watch out. No one steals candy from Cocoa the Chocolate Fairy!"

"No!" Raina blurted out. "No fairy has ever been on the other side of the Frosted Mountains! Our magic doesn't work over there."

"You don't know that for sure," Berry pointed out.

"Come on, Raina," Cocoa said. "We don't know if all those stories are true."

Raina's eyes grew wide with panic. "You don't believe the Fairy Code Book? Are you nuts?" Raina, unlike her friends, had memorized the Fairy Code Book. She knew the entire history of Candy Kingdom, and she was quick to point out any dangers.

Melli put her hand on Raina's shoulder. "Raina has a point. Have you ever heard of any fairy going far beyond Chocolate River and over the Frosted Mountains?"

"Why would anyone want to?" Dash cracked. "Everything we need is here—well, except the eggs, I guess."

Cocoa closed her eyes. "Bittersweet chocolate,"

she moaned. "This is awful." Her wings drooped low on the ground.

"Don't dip your wings in syrup yet," Berry said calmly. "We can think of a plan."

"Yes," Cocoa agreed. She was starting to perk up a little. "A plan to get me to Mogu's bridge. I've got a few words for him."

Berry held up her hand. "All right, hold on," she said. "You can't just go flying out there by yourself."

Raina's face was full of concern. "A fairy can't take anything from under a troll's bridge without permission," she said. She noticed the surprised looks on her friends' faces. "You really haven't read the Fairy Code Book?" she asked.

Laughing, Berry shook her head. "We don't have to," she said. "We have you!"

"Very funny," Raina said. "But this is serious sugar."

"There's only one person who can help," Melli said gently. Her friends nodded in agreement. They were all thinking the same thing.

Cocoa knew exactly who Melli was thinking of, but she didn't want to say. How could she tell the sweet fairy princess such awful news?

"Princess Lolli has a heart of sugar," Raina reminded her. "She'll be able to help. She is the wisest fairy in the kingdom."

"They don't call her princess for nothing," Dash added.

Berry moved closer to Cocoa. "She's your best bet, Cocoa. If anyone can hatch a plan to get the eggs back, it's Princess Lolli."

Cocoa knew her friends were right. Princess

Lolli always knew what to do. But would the princess let her go to Black Licorice Swamp? Cocoa had to go rescue the eggs—even if it meant she had to cross the Frosted Mountains alone!

6

A Chocolate Promise

The fairies took off in the air and headed to Candy Castle. They flew side by side. They were on a mission to help their friend Cocoa.

Cocoa felt so lucky to have such good, true friends. She hoped with all her heart that no one else noticed the empty chocolate nest. Facing the other Chocolate Fairies would be terrible. She had to get those eggs back from Mogu before the parade!

When they could see the tallest lollipops in Lollipop Landing, Cocoa slowed her wings.

"Wait, what should I say to the princess?" Cocoa asked her friends. She floated in the air, waiting for the fairies to reply. "She has to let me go save the eggs!"

Her friends gathered around her.

Melli took her hand. "You should tell Princess Lolli the truth," she told her. "That's the easiest thing to do."

"And the hardest," Berry added.

"We'll all be with you," Raina said, reaching out to hold her friend's hand.

Dash bobbed her head up and down. "We won't leave your side," she vowed. "Plus, not only is Princess Lolli the kindest fairy, she's the smartest. She'll know what to do."

"Come on," Melli said. She squeezed Cocoa's hand, and together they flew off.

Cocoa was thankful for Melli's warm grip. While she wasn't afraid to find Mogu, she couldn't help being nervous about telling Princess Lolli what had happened. How would the princess react? She had put her trust in Cocoa. And Cocoa had made a solid chocolate promise to care for the eggs. Now that promise was broken.

"Everything will be okay," Melli said, looking over at Cocoa. "Princess Lolli won't be mad. She'll know this isn't your fault. Don't worry."

"We're almost there," Raina called out.

The bright pink castle came into view. With

her friends by her side, Cocoa felt she could handle anything. She would simply tell the princess that she had to save the eggs!

In front of the castle the Royal Gardens were in full bloom. All the brightly colored candy looked gorgeous—and delicious!

The garden was the pride of Sugar Valley. There was a sampling of all the candy grown in the kingdom, from the smallest fruit chews to the largest peppermint sticks. It was a rainbow of colors and a sensational sight.

The Castle Fairies who took care of the Royal Garden candy were all busy at work. They didn't even look up to wonder why the five Candy Fairies were flying in through the sugarcoated gates.

"Good afternoon," a fairy guard said, greeting them. He wore the official white-and-pink castle uniform. He tipped his cap and smiled. "What brings you lovely fairies here today?"

"Hello," Cocoa responded bravely. "We're here to see Princess Lolli."

"Is she expecting you?" the guard asked. He eyed the five fairies carefully.

Cocoa was about to answer, but the words wouldn't come out. She was too embarrassed to admit that the precious eggs were gone! She didn't know what to say to the guard.

Berry stepped forward. She fluttered her long pink wings. "Cocoa is the Chocolate Fairy watching over the spring eggs," she said. "She needs to speak to the princess at once."

While Cocoa didn't like people speaking for her, she was very relieved that Berry had stepped in. She turned to her friend and smiled. She was thankful that her friend understood how hard this was for her.

The guard nodded his head, and two Royal Fairies blew their shiny caramel trumpets to announce their arrival. Then the guard lifted the heavy white chocolate gate, and the fairies flew inside.

Cocoa took a deep breath as her feet touched down on the red licorice bridge. As she and her friends crossed the chocolate moat, Cocoa grew even more concerned. She looked around at all the candy in the Royal Gardens. If Mogu was able to send the Chuchies over to get the chocolate eggs, what would stop him from taking more candy? The whole kingdom was in danger! She hoped with all her heart that this egg situation would be fixed. And that she could put a stop to Mogu's candy stealing.

CHAPTER

7

A Dangerous Plan

The five fairies found Princess Lolli in the throne room watering a multiflavored jelly bean plant. She looked up and smiled at her guests.

"Hello," Princess Lolli called. "What a nice surprise to see you all here today." She lifted the heavy leaves of the plant. Gently, she plucked

a few ripe beans. "Would you care for some fresh jelly beans? The green apple and grape are especially tasty."

Cocoa stepped forward. "No, thank you, Princess Lolli," she said. "We're here with some very bitter news."

Looking concerned, the princess placed the golden watering can down. She waved the fairies into her chamber. There was a pink throne bejeweled with little pieces of dazzling sugar candies, and there were pink velvet couches for visitors. "Come inside," she told them. "Tell me what has happened. You all have such sour faces!"

The fairies followed the princess into the room. Before they even sat down on the princess's regal couches, Cocoa blurted out, "The chocolate eggs have been stolen from the nest in Chocolate Woods!"

"Stolen?" Princess Lolli asked. She sat in her throne. Her face no longer showed a smile, but a frown.

"Yes, princess," Berry said. She moved closer to her. "Raina and I saw a bunch of Chuchies taking the eggs across the river."

The princess touched her wavy strawberry-colored hair. "Mogu," she whispered.

"That's what we think," Dash piped up.

"Oh, princess!" Raina cried out. "Cocoa wants to cross the Frosted Mountains! I told her that it wasn't safe, but she still wants to go!"

Cocoa smiled at Raina. She knew her friend was just nervous for her. "The eggs were my responsibility," Cocoa said bravely. "I made a promise to protect the eggs. I want to go get them back." She stood up and walked closer to the candy throne. "The chocolate eggs mean so much to all of Candy Kingdom," she pleaded. "The Egg Parade is in two days!"

Princess Lolli looked thoughtfully at Cocoa. "Traveling across the Frosted Mountains is a dangerous journey," she warned.

"I know," Cocoa replied. She lowered her head. "But I need to go. The eggs were my responsibility. And now the kingdom is in great danger!"

"Your magic may not be as strong on the other side of the mountains," Princess Lolli went on. She looked into Cocoa's sad brown eyes. "As we head over the Frosted Mountains, our magic gets weaker."

"I understand," Cocoa told her. "But I want

to get those eggs back. We need to put a stop to Mogu's stealing."

The five fairies waited for the princess to respond. They gathered around Cocoa, holding hands. They stood in silence as they watched the princess decide.

The beautiful fairy princess looked out the large window of her chambers. She was deep in thought. When she finally turned back to look at them, she chose her words carefully.

"Mogu can't get away with stealing our candy," Princess Lolli said, full of determination. "We have to put a stop to this."

"I was hoping you'd say that," Cocoa said. She smiled at the princess.

"We will go together," Princess Lolli told her.

"Just the two of us. The trip is too dangerous to take you all."

Cocoa's friends looked worried. They wanted to help too. But Princess Lolli's decision was final.

Cocoa clapped her hands. *"Choc-o-rific!"* she cheered. "Wait till I get my hands on Mogu. . . ."

Princess Lolli held up her hand. "Wait," she said. "You will need to follow my every word. The only way to get what we want is to trick Mogu. Tricking an old troll like Mogu is sticky business. We will have to be clever and wise."

Cocoa nodded her head. "I understand," she told the princess.

"Mogu has tried to steal candy before," Princess Lolli said. "But he has never stolen chocolate eggs."

"I guess now he's got the Chuchies to do his dirty work for him," Berry said.

"All the more reason to teach him a lesson before the Chuchies become a bigger problem," Princess Lolli told them.

Raina took a map from her bag. "Here," she said. She gave the old scroll to the princess. "It's a map I drew of the Frosted Mountains. I memorized the locations from the Fairy Code Book. I hope it helps you reach Black Licorice Swamp safely."

Princess Lolli touched Raina's head gently. "Thank you," she said. "That map will be very useful." She looked each fairy in the eye. "I don't want all the fairies in the kingdom to panic," she explained. "This needs to remain a secret for now.

Can I count on all of you to keep this quiet?"

The fairies all nodded their heads solemnly.

"We will be back before Sun Dip," the princess said. "And, hopefully, we will return with the chocolate eggs."

Cocoa wanted to believe the princess. She hoped that by going on this journey, they would get the eggs back. And stop Mogu from stealing more from the fairies. It was a dangerous plan. Now more than ever she knew she had to be brave.

8

Black Licorice

"A re you ready, Cocoa?" Princess Lolli asked. She stood at the back chocolate gate of the Candy Castle.

Cocoa nodded her head. She had no idea what the journey would be like, or what would happen. She hugged each of her friends.

"Be safe," Raina told her.

"Watch your wings," Berry advised. "Trolls are sneaky."

"Thanks," Cocoa said. She turned to Dash. "I'll see you soon."

"You better!" Dash called out.

Melli stood off to the side. She was trying to be brave like her friends. She didn't want to get all gooey; Cocoa wouldn't like that. Still, it was hard for her to be strong as she watched her friend fly into danger.

"We'll be all right," Cocoa told her. She gave Melli a tight squeeze. Cocoa didn't like to see her upset. "Save some of your caramel sticks for me," she said. "We'll be back for Sun Dip."

Melli managed to smile. "Sure as sugar," she whispered.

Princess Lolli reached out for Cocoa's hand.

Together, they flew off over the Royal Gardens to Red Licorice Lake. Cocoa watched as a bunch of fairies cared for the licorice growing around the cherry-red lake. They were all laughing as they trimmed the thick, sweet stalks.

As she flew, thoughts raced through her head. *What if we can't get the eggs back? What if something happens to Princess Lolli?*

When Peppermint Grove came into view, Cocoa tried to push those thoughts out of her head. She had to be strong. Chocolate River was up ahead. She had only been on the other side of the river once, last winter. She had gone to Marshmallow Marsh to gather filling for chocolate squares. The marsh was sticky, but not a scary place at all. Not like Black Licorice Swamp! Cocoa could feel her heart beating faster.

The rumbling of the river interrupted her thoughts. The flight over the river was quick. Cocoa looked down on the fluffy white peaks of Marshmallow Marsh. In a few quick wing strokes, they would be sailing up over the Frosted Mountains.

Cocoa looked at the princess. "What is the plan?" she asked.

Princess Lolli smiled and winked at the Chocolate Fairy. "We just need to stay true to our hearts. Salty old Mogu might be sneaky, but he isn't always wise."

Cocoa wanted to believe the princess. Still, she was unsure how the two of them could battle the old troll. In the stories she had heard as a young fairy, the troll was sneaky and strong. How could two small fairies be a match for him?

"Have you ever met Mogu?" Cocoa asked.

"Once," Princess Lolli replied. "I was a young fairy working with a crop of marshmallow blossoms at the edge of the marsh. Mogu thought he could trick me into giving him my basket of candy."

Cocoa flapped her wings to get closer to the princess. "Were you scared?"

"No," the princess said. "I knew I could outsmart him." She grinned and adjusted the silver crown on her head. "And I did!"

The Frosted Mountains were straight ahead. Cocoa took a deep breath.

"Remember," Princess Lolli told her, "our powers are not as strong on this side of the mountains. We will need to use our magic wisely."

Suddenly Cocoa felt dizzy. She closed her eyes for a second.

"Cocoa, hold on," Princess Lolli said, gripping Cocoa's hand tighter. "I know this trip is very difficult."

Feeling the princess's hand squeeze hers made her feel much better. All at once Cocoa had a burst of energy. When she opened her eyes again, she saw that the princess was smiling.

"The air here makes it hard for fairies to breathe," Princess Lolli said kindly. "But stay calm and you'll be fine. Come, let's head down to the swamp and find Mogu. Raina's map says this is the right direction."

Cocoa held tight to Princess Lolli's hand as they sailed over the Black Licorice Swamp. The smell of the thick, gooey swamp made her nose twitch. Everything around the swamp was black. Not at all like Red Licorice Lake. She longed to see the bright red stalks and wild berry candy bushes blooming along the Red Licorice Lake shores, and the happy Red Licorice Fairies harvesting the ripe stalks. Here at the dark, gloomy swamp there was no one in sight.

"Look over there!" Princess Lolli said, pointing.

The princess was pointing to a small bridge at the far end of the swamp. The bridge's black licorice bricks were covered in salt and didn't look very sturdy. Surrounding the bridge were tall, thin pretzel sticks. It looked like no one had cared for the pretzels—or the bridge—in years.

"There it is," Princess Lolli declared. "Mogu's

bridge. He's probably in his cave under the bridge."

"Let's go see," Cocoa said. She felt a new wave of energy and was ready to go.

"Wait," Princess Lolli told her. She held Cocoa back. "Remember, anything that is under the bridge cannot be removed without the troll's permission. We will need to be clever, and quick."

Cocoa nodded her head. "Yes, I remember," she said. She thought of her friends back in Sugar Valley, and tried to be as brave as Princess Lolli. "I'm ready."

Her head was still feeling strange, and Cocoa wondered if she could fly one more inch. But she knew that she had to keep going.

They flew down and hid behind a large black licorice stalk growing near the bridge. Carefully, they stepped over the rough salted pretzel sticks to get a better view of Mogu.

Cocoa gasped and drew her hands quickly up to her mouth. There was Mogu! His skin was wrinkled and dirty, and his clothes were torn. Just as all the stories described him, he was short and stout with white hair in a rim around his round head. And his large nose was sniffing one of Cocoa's chocolate eggs!

C H A P T E R

9

Chocolate Dreams

Princess Lolli and Cocoa stood together in the shadows of Mogu's bridge. The air was misty and cold, and the two fairies huddled close. Quietly, they peered around the salty old licorice bricks.

Cocoa couldn't believe how close she was to the troll! She found that she was less scared now that she saw him. She clutched her fists close to her side. She had to get those eggs back home!

Mogu was lying lazily on a hammock strung up under the bridge. The eggs were laid out in a black licorice basket before him.

Cocoa wanted to reach out and take the eggs, but she knew that she had to wait for Princess Lolli's instructions. She leaned closer to hear what Mogu was saying.

"Ah, I've missed the smell of chocolate," he grumbled. He rolled over and put his large nose ncxt to the eggs and breathed deeply. "Ahhhh," he sighed.

Four Chuchies were sitting around the basket. Their round pom-pom bodies shook as they jumped up and down on their short, thin legs. "Meee, meee, meeeeeeeee," they chanted in a high-pitched squeal.

"Yes," Mogu said, petting one Chuchie. "I know you want to eat one." He grinned, showing off his black teeth. "You did a great job of getting these eggs over the mountains."

"Heee heee heeeeeeeeeeeeee," the Chuchies cried out together.

Mogu looked pleased. "Yes, this was a ghoulish plan," he said. He shifted his weight in his hammock. "Those fairies never would have imagined that I could steal these eggs." His short arms rose up above his head. "Everyone knows spring eggs are the sweetest chocolate." He stretched happily. A sly grin spread across his face. "One day all the chocolate in the valley will be ours!"

Cocoa's eyes grew wide. How could Mogu be so cruel? She felt Princess Lolli squeeze her

hand. It was getting hard to stay quiet and listen to the mean troll.

"I've had enough of all those happy fairies and their sweetness in Sugar Valley," Mogu went on. He swung his short legs around to the side of the hammock and stood up. "This candy was so easy to take, just sitting in the nest! And no one was even watching! Why shouldn't we take more?"

Because we work hard to make the chocolate and all the candy in the valley, Cocoa wanted to scream. *Stealing is not the way to get candy!* She wanted to scold the troll. She bit her lip to keep quiet. Looking over at Princess Lolli, she wondered how the princess was remaining so calm. Now more than ever she wanted to reach out for the eggs.

"When I am the ruler of Candy Kingdom," Mogu bragged, "things will be different." He stomped his feet as he marched around the basket of eggs. He puffed his chest out. "I have big chocolate dreams." He kneeled down next to the basket. He stroked the eggs. "Hmmm," he said, sighing. Turning to the Chuchies, he grinned. "I will rule over the entire valley, my furry friends. And we will have all the chocolate that we could ever dream of! *Bah-ha-haaaaaaaa!*"

Bittersweet chocolate! Cocoa wanted to cry out. What would happen to all the sweet fairies in Sugar Valley if Mogu were in charge? What would happen to Candy Castle and Princess Lolli? This was all too horrible to think about. Defeated, Cocoa sank down to the soft, gooey ground of the swamp. What were they going to do?

Just then she felt a gentle squeeze on her shoulder. Princess Lolli was standing tall next to her. She had a slight grin on her face.

Cocoa knew that Princess Lolli had come up with a plan. She could tell from the sparkle in her eyes. But would the plan be strong enough to outwit this selfish troll? Would they be able to get the eggs safely home? Cocoa's wings fluttered. She was ready to do whatever the princess asked of her.

A Touch of Chocolate

Princess Lolli waved Cocoa away from the bridge. They stood off to the side of the swamp so they could whisper.

"This is not your fault, Cocoa," Princess Lolli told her. "Mogu was wrong. And we will get the eggs back."

Cocoa wanted to believe the princess. She

nodded her head. All she wanted to do was protect those eggs from Mogu. A chocolate promise was a solid vow, and she wanted to be true to her word.

"When the time is right," Princess Lolli said, "I will signal to you." She looked into the fairy's sweet face. "You must concentrate and focus on your task. Because your magic is weaker on this side of the mountains, you need to rely on your heart."

Cocoa was not exactly sure what the princess was asking her to do. She could hardly even fly! But she wanted to help. She listened carefully.

"See the pretzel bramble over there?" the princess asked. She pointed behind Cocoa. "Do you think you can coat the stalks with chocolate?"

Cocoa wasn't sure she would be able to do as

the princess asked. Normally, she could touch anything and it would be covered in chocolate. But her head was spinning and there was a heaviness in her wings. Her magic was much weaker here. She didn't think she could create any chocolate!

Slowly Cocoa reached out to touch the pretzel stick. The pointy salt crystals were rough on her fingertips. Closing her eyes, she drew her breath in. When she opened her eyes, the salt was still there. There was not a drop of chocolate in sight. Cocoa's wings drooped low, and she looked down at her feet.

"Cocoa, you can do this," the princess told her. "Try again. Think of Chocolate Falls and Chocolate Woods. Listen to your heart."

This time Cocoa took a moment to think of her

home. She raised her head and closed her eyes. She thought of the ripples in Chocolate River and the rumbling sounds of Chocolate Falls. She imagined the dark bark of the old chocolate oak, and the tiny, strong chocolate branches of the egg nest. She remembered the sweet smell of chocolate rising throughout Sugar Valley on a beautiful spring day. Soon she imagined she could actually smell real chocolate.

"Oh, Cocoa!" Princess Lolli cried out.

Cocoa opened her eyes. The pretzels were now coated with rich, dark chocolate. Gently swaying in the breeze was a bunch of chocolate-covered pretzel sticks!

"You did it!" the princess said proudly. "I knew you had a solid chocolate heart!" She grinned. "You are a brave and true Candy Fairy, Cocoa."

The princess hugged her tightly. "Stay here until I call for you," she said.

In a flash, the royal fairy was gone.

Cocoa watched as the princess bravely stepped forward from the shadows of the bridge.

"Hello, Mogu," she said calmly. "I think you have something that belongs to Candy Kingdom."

Mogu turned his head, and Cocoa saw the surprised look on his face. "Well, well. Princess Lolli," he said. He quickly got over the shock of seeing the fairy princess and laughed. His laughter shook the whole bridge.

"What, these eggs? *Bah-ha-haaaaaaaa!* Your magic is no good here," he spat. "You know that you cannot move these eggs unless I allow it." He chuckled to himself. "And that is *not* going to

happen! I am in the mood for some chocolate."

The princess nodded her head knowingly. "Well then, I have something for you," she said. "Cocoa, show Mogu what you made." Bravely, Cocoa flew under the bridge with her arms full of the chocolate-covered pretzels.

Mogu's eyes grew big when he saw what the Candy Fairy was carrying. He took the sticks and shoved them all in his mouth. "Mmm," he said with his mouth full. "Salty and sweet! More! More!"

"As you wish," Princess Lolli said. She motioned for Cocoa to make more chocolate-covered pretzels.

The troll laughed. "You are going to give me candy?" he asked. He laughed as he reached out to grab the chocolate from Cocoa. "This is easier than I thought!"

The greedy troll kept on eating. Cocoa was getting weaker and weaker with each batch that she made. But the troll went on eating up all the chocolate treats. The Chuchies scurried around his feet, grabbing at all the crumbs that fell from his mouth. They were giddy with chocolate joy.

Cocoa wasn't sure why the princess was being so nice to Mogu. After all, he had stolen from them! Why would she want to give him more? But whatever the reason, she hoped with all her heart that the princess's chocolate plan worked.

11

Dark Chocolate Wishes

Standing in the shadows of Mogu's cave, Cocoa watched. With Cocoa's help, the gentle fairy princess gave Mogu all the chocolate-covered pretzel sticks he wanted. Now his face was stained with chocolate. His hands were covered in a melted brown mess. The more he grabbed the chocolate and shoved it in his mouth, the more the princess grinned—and the dirtier he became.

"Mmmm," Mogu hummed. "I want more! I want more!"

Cocoa trusted Princess Lolli, but she wondered why she was giving Mogu the chance to eat so much chocolate.

"When I rule Candy Kingdom," he boasted. "I will make sure there are plenty of these salty chocolate treats. Thanks for the idea, princess! *Bah-ha-haaaaaaaa!*"

Mogu's evil laugh ruffled Cocoa's wings. She leaned against the bridge's salty black licorice bricks. Making the chocolate had taken most of her energy. And being on the far side of the Frosted Mountains was taking a toll on her. She tried hard to stand quiet and still.

Cocoa looked over at Princess Lolli. The brave princess was standing next to Mogu's hammock, watching him stuff himself with the chocolate treats. She caught Cocoa's eye and winked.

Then Cocoa heard the cry.

"Ooooooooh," moaned Mogu. He stumbled back toward his hammock.

Princess Lolli moved out of the way.

Mogu sat down. His hands were on his bulging belly. "Ooooh, my tummy," he wailed.

The Chuchies crowded around him. "Mee, mee, meeeeeeeeeee?" they chanted together.

Princess Lolli offered him another bundle of chocolate-covered pretzels. Mogu waved his hand in front of his face. "Let me be!" he shouted. He moaned louder. "No more chocolate!" he mumbled. He closed his eyes and leaned back in the hammock.

"Mee, mee, *MEEEEEEEEE*?" the Chuchies asked a little louder.

Cocoa moved closer to Princess Lolli to get a better look. The damp cave now smelled like chocolate. Princess Lolli held up her hand, signaling Cocoa to wait.

"Argh!" the troll barked. He opened one eye. He peered over at the stack of chocolate pretzel sticks lying on the floor. He pushed the pretzels and the basket of eggs away with his foot.

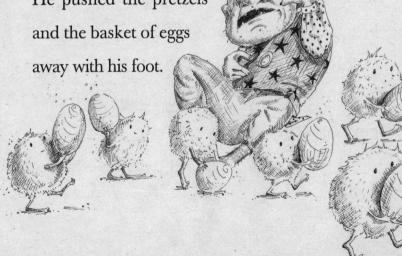

"No more chocolate! Take all the chocolate away! I don't want to see chocolate under this bridge anymore!"

The Chuchies jumped up and got to work. When Mogu gave an order, they moved!

Princess Lolli stepped back and took Cocoa's hand. The Chuchies lifted the chocolate egg basket. They set the basket on the muddy ground—away from the bridge.

The eggs were no longer under the bridge!

Princess Lolli and Cocoa had tricked the troll without his realizing! He had ordered the eggs to be moved from under his bridge.

"Mogu," Princess Lolli said softly. She walked over to the hammock, where the troll was groaning softly.

"Is he asleep?" Cocoa whispered. She

peered over Princess Lolli's shoulder.

"Not quite," the princess told her. "But he will be in a chocolate coma for a while. He ate more than his fair share of chocolate today. His greed was almost as big as his appetite!"

Cocoa giggled. "And he had a very big appetite!"

"Oh, my tummy," Mogu cried out. He rolled over uncomfortably in his hammock.

Princess Lolli leaned in closer to him. "Nothing good comes of stealing, Mogu," she said.

Mogu moaned again.

"The sweet candy that you had today was freely given to you, and therefore the best kind," Princess Lolli told him. "But be warned," she said. "You must ask for candy, and never steal."

The Chuchies scrambled for all the chocolate

crumbs left spread around on the ground. They didn't look up as Princess Lolli and Cocoa slipped away from the bridge.

Princess Lolli turned to Cocoa. "Come, let's get the eggs back to the nest," she said. "Mogu won't be bothering us for a while now."

"Are you sure?" Cocoa asked. She looked back at the troll.

Mogu grunted and rolled over. "No more chocolate," he muttered in his sleep. "No more. . . ." Soon he was snoring heavily.

"Yes," Princess Lolli said, smiling. She took both of Cocoa's hands and held them tight. "You were very brave today, Cocoa. I am so proud of you. I know it wasn't easy for you to make those chocolate pretzel sticks. That took strength and courage."

Cocoa blushed. "Thank you, princess," she said. "I can't help but feel this was my fault. I gave you my promise to take care of these eggs. Plus, I couldn't let Mogu take over Sugar Valley!"

"And he won't," Princess Lolli said. "At least, not today!" Her eyes sparkled. "Best to trick a troll with sweetness," she added. "There are other ways, but this is the surest."

The two fairies hugged.

"Come, let's bring the eggs home," Princess Lolli said. "We'll be back just in time for Sun Dip."

Together, they lifted the basket and flew the eggs back to the chocolate nest.

12

Solid Chocolate

Wow!" Melli whispered to Cocoa. "Everything does look *choc-o-rific*! You saved the day, Cocoa."

Cocoa and her friends stood on a stage built of white chocolate in the Royal Gardens. A large white banner hung across the stage. WELCOME, SPRING! was written in pink icing letters. Huge baskets of delicious candy flowers and thick red licorice stalks made the stage a beautiful sight. Everyone in the Royal Gardens was waiting for the Egg Parade to reach the castle. And to get a glimpse of the chocolate eggs!

Cheers were heard throughout the kingdom as the Chocolate Fairies marched in the festive parade. Some fairies rode on large floats made of chocolate, from the darkest dark to the purest white chocolate. On each float there were fairies showing off the season's chocolate treats. Other Chocolate Fairies marched alongside the floats, waving and throwing out candy to the crowd.

The cheers brought a smile to Cocoa's face. The Egg Parade was a big success, and the prized eggs were definitely the highlight.

"Everything does look *choc-o-rific!*" Cocoa said,

smiling. She looked around at her friends. "Sure as sugar this wouldn't have happened if it weren't for all of you."

"We didn't do anything," Dash said. "You were the one who saved the kingdom!"

"No fairy has ever been able to create candy in Black Licorice Swamp!" Raina cried.

Berry laughed. "Not that any fairy would want to!"

"The fact is that you did save the eggs," Melli said. "You are a hero, Cocoa!"

"And I have the sweetest friends," Cocoa added. She reached out to hug her friends. "You all came to help. You dropped everything and came to Chocolate Woods. You gave me the courage to go to Princess Lolli. How can I ever thank you?"

"That's what friends do," Raina said simply.

"Sure as sugar, they do!" Melli said, hugging Cocoa. "We are all very proud of you. Really."

"And Princess Lolli," Cocoa added. She looked over at the beautiful fairy princess. She was wearing her crown iced with the prized royal jewels, and her bright pink regal robe. "You should have seen her. She was so clever. She never gave in to that salty old troll! Her plan worked perfectly."

Just then the caramel trumpets blared. Everyone looked to the royal gates. The candy procession slowly made its way up a special red walkway made of the finest strawberry and raspberry candies. The Chocolate Fairies all beamed with pride as they walked to the stage.

Princess Lolli sat tall in her dazzling candy throne in the middle of the stage. The Royal

Fairies had worked so hard to make the castle sparkle, and everything was perfect. Princess Lolli waved Cocoa over to her.

Cocoa flew over excitedly.

"It's almost time," Princess Lolli said. She smiled warmly at the Chocolate Fairy. "Are you ready, Cocoa?"

"I am," Cocoa said, full of pride. She leaned in closer and whispered in her ear, "Thank you, princess."

Cocoa stood tall next to Princess Lolli's throne. She straightened her special chocolate leaf crown on her head. She was ready. Feeling like her heart would burst with happiness, she tried to keep her wings still.

Four Chocolate Fairies carried a large sugar basket up to the stage. A chocolate quilt covered the spring eggs inside.

Princess Lolli stepped to the front of the stage. "Welcome to the annual Egg Parade!" she announced. She smiled at the crowd of fairies that filled the Royal Gardens.

The fairies all cheered.

"It is with great pride that I call upon Cocoa, our bravest Chocolate Fairy," she said. "She has the honor of unveiling the prized spring chocolate eggs. Without her bravery, strength, and solid chocolate heart, we would not have these special eggs to celebrate today!"

An excited roar erupted from the crowd. The fairies were chanting Cocoa's name. Word had spread quickly of Cocoa's bravery. Everyone in Sugar Valley knew how Cocoa had made chocolate-covered pretzels appear in the Black Licorice Swamp and how she had helped put an end to Mogu's plan. The chanting grew louder as she reached the center of the stage.

Cocoa stood next to Princess Lolli, waving to the crowd. Then she looked back over her shoulder. Her friends were cheering. Never had she been so proud!

She took hold of the chocolate blanket covering the sugar basket. With a gentle tug the blanket came off. Sparkling in the bright sunlight were the chocolate eggs. They were wrapped in the special foil covers created by the Royal Foil Fairies. The brightly colored designs were bold and beautiful. Each one had a unique design. The Royal Foil Fairies had done a fantastic job. The eggs were a delicious sight!

The crowd gasped. This was the highlight of the Egg Parade! And no one was happier than Cocoa.

"Cheers for Cocoa!" Princess Lolli declared. "Her bravery and her dedication to these eggs are reasons to celebrate. Happy Spring to all the fairies of Sugar Valley!"

The cheers brought a huge smile to Cocoa's face.

"And now," the princess declared, "let the chocolate feast begin!"

"I thought she'd never say that!" Dash said happily. She flew off quickly to gather some of the chocolate treats.

"Come on," Berry urged her friends. "Let's check out the floats with all the chocolates!" She spread her pink wings and followed Dash.

Cocoa took Melli's and Raina's hands. "You heard the princess," she said. "Let's eat!"

Together, the three fairies flew after Dash and Berry into the crowd.

The caramel trumpets blasted once again. Spring had arrived—along with the most delicious chocolates ever grown in Sugar Valley.

Cocoa watched her friends enjoying the feast. They gathered around her, grinning. Standing together, they all felt the excitement of the day.

Candy Kingdom was safe from Mogu—for now, at least. And that was definitely a reason for a sweet celebration.

Helen Perelman enjoys candy from all parts of Sugar Valley, but jelly beans, red licorice, and gummy fish are her favorites. She worked in a children's bookstore and was a children's book editor . . . but, sadly, she never worked in a candy store. She now writes full time in New York City, where she lives with her husband and two daughters.